D1565235

The Art of the

BonsaiPotato ™

by
Jeffrey E. Fitzsimmons

illustrations
Mike Dillon

photography
Jim Linna

The Art of the

Bonsai Potato
™

ISBN 0-9664741-4-7

For information contact
sensei@bonsaipotato.com

TABLE OF CONTENTS

"Often it is the one with the most eyes who cannot see."

– Zen Proverb

Are you a person who longs for patience and tranquility in your life? Of course you are, but in our modern society who has the time?

Now it's possible. With the techniques contained within this book you can quickly and efficiently reach an inner peace that can take monks an entire lifetime to achieve. The secrets are now yours.

Zen - Without the wait!™

Welcome to
The Art of the Bonsai Potato™

INTRODUCTION

A Brief History Of Bonsai*

Bonsai trees were not always the tiny trees that we see today. Fossilized remains of prehistoric bonsai trees suggest that they once grew to nearly 60 feet tall and lived to be centuries old.

Smaller living versions growing to heights of 20 to 30 feet known as Qi guai mei shu were recorded in China as recently as 5000 years ago. A traveler named Po Chu-yi was passing through Yuan pu where these majestic trees flourished. He was so impressed with their beauty that he wanted to take one back to his home and plant it for all to enjoy.

The trees were so large in their adult state that he decided to uproot a number of saplings and transport them home. Once home he dedicated many hours every day caring for the young trees. He watered and pruned them daily but couldn't get them to grow more than two feet tall. After seven years he discarded his early efforts and returned to Yuan pu to harvest a new batch.

*The title claims that this is a brief history, but that can be relative. This version of Potato Bonsai™ history is actually a couple of pages long. Since this is only the first step down the shortcut to patience, you may want to read this a little at a time to maintain interest. If you have no interest whatsoever in the rich history of the Bonsai Potato™ and want to jump right in, by all means go ahead, but remember, "A person formed by cutting corners only appears well-rounded."

After spending time amongst the glorious Qi guai mei shu trees, his spirit was renewed and he left determined to make his new plants flourish.

His new efforts produced the same results. He reasoned that because the adult trees were incredibly old they must have a tremendously protracted growth cycle and spent the next 20 years of his life meticulously maintaining the trees. Over the years his impatience grew as much as his trees didn't, so as Mr. Po was getting to be an old man he decided to find someone to continue caring for the trees upon his death.

Po Chu-yi didn't have a family (a young tree requires more attention than one would generally think) so Chu-yi decided on Emperor Huang because of his renowned gardens and his love for botany. Chu-yi requested an audience with Emperor Huang to present him with the trees. Seeing Emperor Huang's gardens Chu-yi realized that he had chosen wisely. He had never seen gardens more painstakingly maintained. Unfortunately, Chu-yi underestimated Emperor Huang's love for nature. Only one week previous he had proclaimed that the majestic Qi guai mei shu was a natural treasure and a sacred plant. Chu-yi stood before Emperor Huang with his potted plants like so many heads on platters.

Emperor Huang regarded this as an act of aggression and had him quickly beheaded.*

Rather than let all the trees go to waste Emperor Huang decided to keep them for himself. He became fascinated with their intricacies and found the hours working on them to be extremely relaxing. He began to give them away as gifts to his friends and the little trees soon became a status symbol among the ruling class. The commoners also enjoyed the trees but they were forced to use more readily available (and less sacred) trees like Juniper and Elm.

It was later discovered that the Qi guai mei shu trees grew only 12-20 inches in the first 400 years of their lives but at exactly 400 years they experienced a growth spurt of up to 24 feet. Unfortunately for Emperor Huang, his trees were not saplings but nearly 400 years old. Within a 24 hour period all of the trees "leapt from their pots like (untranslateable Chinese simile)." The growth spurt killed the entire ruling class as their palaces collapsed upon them.

The common people gathered, decided that nobody wanted to rule, and abandoned the dynasty due to lack of interest. They went their separate ways...

...but they took their trees with them.

*Note: In 1983 forensic archeologists working with a BBC film crew shooting a documentary entitled 'Big Man Little Tre e s exhumed his body. After a series of autopsies and expensive computer simulations they determined that he actually died of natural causes a split-second before he was beheaded.

The practice of what has come to be known as Bonsai spread throughout China. The art form became extremely popular amongst traders and Buddhist monks in Japan once trade relations were established.

The Irish Connection

In 925 Ireland decided to send emissaries to Japan to study their art and culture, and integrate it into their own. The plan was poorly funded and low priority but eventually they found a single volunteer. Young Kieran McGlynn traveled through Japan for eight years gathering information.

Upon his return the people of Ireland found that Mr. McGlynn had "poorer than average recollection" but he spoke constantly of "stunted plants displaying incredible beauty and providing great tranquility in their cultivation." When asked how they were created he couldn't recall exactly but he vowed to eventually recreate them. He started cultivating the local plants to reproduce the results and discovered that the most successful one was also the most available; the potato. His experiments revolutionized the art of Bonsai.

Mr. McGlynn found that by using potatoes not only could he create astonishing results in months rather than decades but the plants didn't require re-potting, fertilizer or even water. The art of the Bonsai Potato™ was born!

Bonsai Potato™ art quickly spread throughout Ireland. In the early 1300's references to the Bonsai Potato™ altar began to appear in writings and paintings. An illustration from 1311 depicting Bonsai Potato™ master Robert MacDonald working in his studio (figure I-1) from 1311 is the earliest known record of such an altar and he is widely credited with its creation.

Figure I-1
Robert MacDonald
Circa 1311

Exiled from his native Scotland, Robert MacDonald became one of the most prolific Bonsai Potato™ artists in the history of the art form.

The art of the Bonsai Potato™ thrived for nearly 1000 years but was almost entirely wiped out in the mid-1800's as a result of the Great Irish Potato Famine.

Survival was more important than art and the wave of emigration that accompanied the famine washed nearly every trace of the ancient art form away with it.

Over one hundred years later a small faction of Bonsai Potato™ artists has surfaced in a small town called Spirit Lake, Idaho. As a result, the secrets of tranquility, inner peace and artistic expression are once again available to the world.

SECTION 1

ZEN and the Art of Bonsai

In a simplified form, Zen is a journey to the mind through spiritual enlightenment and physical meditation.

Throughout history Bonsai cultivation has provided people with a tremendous source of tranquility and inner harmony. Traditional bonsai requires acute attention to detail, patience, and discipline. These qualities are perfect for Zen meditation because they remove the artist from the body by introducing a larger time-scale for the mind to function in.

One day a Zen master was visited by his student who asked, "Master, how long will it take for me to attain enlightenment?"

The master looked at him and paused. For three days they stood and stared at each other until finally the master spoke.

"Do you feel enlightened?"

The student carefully considered this and replied, "No."

"Then it will take longer than that."

SECTION 2

ZEN and the Art of the Bonsai Potato™

In the modern world things are different. Nobody has time for discipline, patience and nonsensical allegories about people who obviously don't have jobs! There just isn't enough time.

Picture this scenario.

One day Frank from the finance assessment committee walks into his boss' office.

"Hey Tom, how long do you think it will take for me to become a vice president?"

Tom stands, looking Frank in the eyes for 10 minutes. Finally the phone rings, interrupting Frank's pleas of, "Are you O.K. Tom?" Tom picks up the phone. It's his boss.

"Tom! Where the hell are you!? I've been sitting in this meeting for five minutes talking in circles and looking like an idiot! I need the numbers on the Emerald account!"

Tom whispers into the phone,

"Not now! I'm teaching Frank a lesson about patience."

"Here's your lesson about patience! Why don't you go wait in line at the #!*%@! unemployment office! You're fired!"

What does this story say? It says that even though we may be committed to patience the unfortunate reality is that we don't have time to give it our full attention.

The art of the Bonsai Potato™ can change all of that. You can achieve inner peace in less than ten minutes a week.

In this book you will discover that nothing could be more simple than cultivating a Bonsai Potato™. This is a living plant that doesn't need soil, fertilization, water, or even sunlight! If you choose your Bonsai Potato™ wisely it will literally grow itself.

You still get to benefit from ancient Zen techniques, but in a more modern, timesaving context. This enables you to dedicate as little time as possible to self-enlightenment, and more time to the things that really matter—like television.

SECTION 3

Choosing your potato

When walking over hot coals with bare feet the first step is very important. The same is true with selecting the proper potato for your Bonsai.

The choosing of the potato is an important and personal time for every Bonsai Potato™ artist. Great care should be taken to assure that your vital energies are in order to enable you to interpret the inner vision of the potato. Remember, you are not controlling the potato, you are merely acting as a means for the potato to accomplish its own artistic destiny. A true Bonsai Potato™ artist will learn to recognize and honor the intentions of the potato.

When shopping for your potato it is best to patronize a 24-hour grocery store in the late evening to avoid distracting crowds. This will give you ample "alone-time" to browse the potato bins.

Varieties

There are many varieties of potatoes available, but for the simplicity this section will only cover the top three for our purposes. These are types that are readily available year-round and, generally speaking, have a stronger inner vision.

Russet
(dubā'kus dilectī)

The Russet is
a great starter potato
because it sprouts relatively quickly, often
producing long, fast-growing "branches" which are
perfect for basic wire manipulation. (See Section 6:
Pruning and Training.) They also have the best
temperament of all potatoes.

Yukon Gold
(pyrītā'to)

A young prospector
named Joe Smith was
working a claim in the Yukon
Territory during the Alaskan gold rush of 1898.
After months of fruitless labor he began to find large
clumps of rounded gold nuggets growing in pockets
away from the main vein of gold in the area. He
collected as many nuggets as he could carry and
headed to town to buy drinks for everyone in the local

saloon to celebrate. Later, after a trip to the bank, he found himself penniless and ashamed because he had tried to deposit almost 200 potatoes into his account. Mr. Smith left town and wandered into the mountains to the southwest with nothing but his withering sanity and the memory of many drunk friends.

He was not alone in his misery. It is widely believed that there wouldn't have been as many people financially devastated by the gold rush if tradition had allowed a trip to the bank before stopping at the saloon. (It is also widely believed that this tradition was started by saloon owners.) As this scene played out over and over again these potatoes came to be known as Fools Gold Potatoes and later Yukon Gold.

The Yukon Gold potatoes are, appropriately, "a little slow." They take time to sprout but the resulting stalks are usually much heartier and beautifully colored.

Baby Red
(tuber'us minorī)

The baby red potatoes get their name because they are small and red. Baby red, or new potatoes, provide good balance as secondary elements in multi-varietal arrangements.

Now that you are familiar with the basic types it is time to connect with individual potatoes in order to start the Bonsai Potato™ process. It is a good idea to select three or four to ensure that you have choices when it comes time to work with them.

STEP 1 - See the potato

The first impression of the potato will in most cases be a visual one. If you feel some other connection with a certain potato before you actually see it you should consider this an exceptional potato. Purchase it and skip to the next section.

Due to individual taste some potatoes will be more aesthetically pleasing to you than others. Find a few that appeal to you visually and set them aside.

Note: Also due to individual taste some people will be unable to find potatoes aesthetically pleasing. If you are one of these people just grab a couple of potatoes, purchase them, and skip to the next section.

Next, look them in the eyes. As with humans (and certain rare flightless birds), the eyes are the windows to the soul. The placement and number of eyes will in part determine the growth pattern of your Bonsai. The sprouts emerge from the eyes, so the more eyes the potato has the more pruning options you will have as your Bonsai begins to develop.

STEP 2 - Feel the potato

Literally, feel the potato. You are searching for one that is firm and not wrinkled. Feel for unusual peaks and valleys to lend character to your Bonsai.

STEP 3 - Be the potato

Interpreting the inner artistic vision of a vegetable is not as easy as it sounds. You need to have intuition, patience, and very open-minded friends.

Hold the potato and draw on your empathy skills to get under its skin and feel what it wants to look like. (The long term psychological effects of this exercise are not well-documented so use caution when 'being the potato'.)

Because the art of the Bonsai Potato™ has only recently been introduced to our culture, not everyone will understand your fascination with potatoes. To avoid persecution (or prosecution), when you get to this point it might be a good idea to purchase the top three or four contenders and 'be the potato' in the privacy of your own home.

A NOTE ON EVIL POTATOES

It is important for you to know that there are good potatoes and evil potatoes. It is not important, however, for you to know the details. Suffice it to say that certain artistic visions should not be realized.

"Bu suan ji yong xiaofu"

 - Chinese saying

(roughly translated)

"Don't count your chickens with a hatchet"

SECTION 4

Starting your Bonsai

Now that you have identified your most promising candidates it is time to start your Bonsai Potato™. The first step is to find a suitable home. A Bonsai Potato™ prefers an area that is dark, warm, and humid. A shallow cave in South America would be perfect, but if that is inconvenient try a drawer in your office desk, a shelf in your closet, or a cupboard in your kitchen. (Above the stove or refrigerator works well.)

If you have a potato that has proven to be extraordinarily promising and you don't feel the need to start others, then you could start your potato on the Bonsai Potato™ altar provided with your kit. (See Section 7: Your Bonsai Potato™ Altar.)

WARNING: When starting the potato on the altar it is important to place the potato in an upright position. **DO NOT PLACE YOUR POTATO UPSIDE DOWN ON THE ALTAR!***

*This is actually a Bonsai Potato™ joke dating back to 1412. It is credited to Bonsai Potato™ master Seamus O'Graaten who, in 1415, was found buried head-first up to his waist. One of his former students later confessed to his murder and was sentenced to death.

Most Bonsai Potato™ artists choose to start many potatoes at once. This is a good idea for several reasons, the least of which is that moving a large number of potatoes from the store to your home helps keep an even distribution of weight on the planet reducing the risk of an irregular orbit.

The primary growth environment can have a great influence on the manifestation of a potato's inner vision. Potatoes that are started alone will tend to form starburst clusters or simple stalks. Placing many potatoes in a bag, box, pile or hollowed out stuffed platypus (large) will encourage the roots to grow around the other potatoes forming longer, more elaborate stalks and a mental state that is more accepting of advanced training methods. (see section 6: Pruning and Training)

Set up your potato(es) in its/their primary growth environment and wait. If you are a control freak this will be an extremely frustrating time for you. For the time being you have done all you can. Remember the old saying "a watched potato never sprouts"*

Caring for and not feeding your Bonsai Potato™

Your Bonsai Potato™ is an island of life. A self contained kit. Inside the skin of your potato is everything it needs to finish it's life cycle. Water and

*An independent research team funded by the department of agriculture has had a potato under constant round-the-clock surveillance since 1963 with no signs of sprouting.

nutrients are carefully rationed from within to produce the most impressive Bonsai Potato™ possible. (surprisingly few people realize that the potato is the second smartest member of the plant kingdom) During this early stage of growth it is best for you to just let go. Your potato knows what to do. If you are a generally flaky person this is probably great news. If, however, you are one of those people who are impatient and have a secret nurturing instinct, now would be a good time to invest in a cactus because your Bonsai Potato™ never needs food and never needs water.

It is O.K. to visit your young potato every couple of days to whisper a few words of encouragement or to sing a song to it, but don't smother it. This is a time of great introspection for your potato. Gentle music or books on tape would be appropriate and since your potato's mind is fully open, this would be an opportune time to teach it a second language (most varieties seem to prefer Spanish)

It will take between 6 and 8 weeks for you to have workable 'branches'.

Note: If you are in an extreme hurry for results, turn to appendix A.

SECTION 5

Types Of Growth

There are a variety of Bonsai Potato™ growth patterns that you should be familiar with. The growth pattern is determined largely by the disposition of each individual potato and not necessarily (as one would think) by the potato. There are hundreds of Bonsai Potato™ growth patterns but the following are the most common.

Starburst Cluster
(plate 5-1)

The starburst cluster is a tightly packed grouping of short stalks (spikes) emerging from a single point. Often a single potato will have two or three starburst clusters. Usually, however, there is one larger dominant cluster containing, at maturity, up to 100 spikes.

Offspring Cluster
(plate 5-2)

The offspring cluster is a formation which includes a number of second generation potatoes growing in tight formation on the surface of the main potato.

Simple Stalk
(plate 5-3)

A simple stalk is one with no main secondary branches. Individual single stalks are common on small baby red and new potatoes.

Starburst Cluster
(plate 5-4)

A simple stalk grouping is two to ten simple stalks growing from one point on the surface of the potato.

Squid Grouping
(plate 5-5)

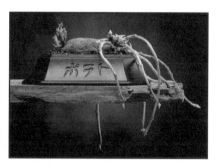

A squid grouping is a cluster with five to twelve single stalks*, each over six inches in length. The 'legs' of a squid grouping can grow to be over 11 inches long. Squid groupings often grow out of single stalk groupings.

---

* Bonsai Potato™ purists prune squid groupings so that they contain only ten 'legs'.

Root Stalk
(plate 5-6)

A root stalk is one that grows up the wall of the potato from the underside. Root stalks can grow alone or in any of the common cluster variations.

Moon Ladder
(plate 5-7)

The Moon Ladder is a dominant stalk with left and right alternating secondary stalks.

Bonsai Potato™ master and poet Sir Angall Flynn (1398-1444) wrote that when his potato sat on the windowsill at night he often felt that he could "...ascend the branches mighty through the still blue light and so on an eve so fair embrace the moon in flight."

"Potato Bonsai™ is a lot like a goose with diarrhea.
You get more out of it than you put into it."

- Gaelic proverb

SECTION 6

Pruning and Training

Before you begin the training process take a deep breath and remember. You are trying to encourage the creativity of the potato. A true Bonsai Potato™ artist learns to respect the inner vision of the potato.

Most potatoes are extremely creative and will become near perfect Bonsai Potatoes™ with little or no outside help.

Having said that, if you find that your particular potato needs a little coaxing, or if your inner vision is slightly different than that of the potato, there are methods at your disposal to 'help' the potato see the big picture.

By this time your potatoes have begun to sprout and you have been chosen by the one which would benefit most from your care. (You may feel as though you have chosen one that you like, but destiny is a subtle matchmaker.)

Once the first sprouts appear you can begin to make basic pruning decisions. If you have small buds appearing from numerous eyes on the potato you should decide which ones will be the primary stalks. and remove the rest. For example, if your potato is producing eight buds from eight different eyes and you only want three main stalks, you should decide which ones will be the three main stalks and remove the other five. In the early stages you can simply pick the small buds off. By doing this you are ensuring that the nutritional resources are being reserved for the primary stalks.

As your primary stalks grow in you will see which growth type your potato is expressing and you can decide on the method of influence you would like to exert. There are limitations to the amount of outside influence a Bonsai Potato™ will accept. For example, it would be traumatic to try to grow a Squid Grouping from a Starburst Cluster. If you push too hard, your Bonsai Potato™ can rebel by dying. (This condition is not reversible)

Pruning
Tools you will need:
- small scissors
- small tweezers

Removing Buds

In order to keep your Bonsai focused you may find it necessary to encourage certain growth patterns and discourage others. The simplest way to do this is to monitor the growth and 'discourage'(i.e. remove) unwanted buds as they develop.

The first indication of growth will be juvenile buds, which are small, tightly-packed leaves that grow out of the eyes of your potato or off of existing stalks. Unwanted juvenile buds can be removed as soon as they appear by pinching them off using a small pair of tweezers. (figure 6-1)

Figure 6-1

Juvenile buds on the surface of your potato can be pinched off with tweezers or can be simply rolled or rubbed off with your finger.

Removing Stalks

Stalks are the individual branches growing out of the surface of your potato. Each surface bud will eventually grow into stalk and the more stalks your potato has the quicker it will deplete its resources.

Often, after your potato has developed to a certain stage you will determine that you have too many stalks for your potato to support or stalks that are improperly oriented. (See Composition p.30). At this point you may opt to remove the unwanted stalks. The best way to do this is to trim the stalk off 1/4"from the surface of the potato. Within a few days the resulting stump will shrivel up and can be easily pinched off. Not only will this remove the stalk, but the follow up will give you a sense of involvement with your potato. If you are entering a competition and need a finished look in a jury (or don't care about developing a relationship with your potato) stalks can be removed by grabbing them firmly at the base and slowly twisting them until they detach.

Removing Branches

Any growths radiating from a main stalk are considered branches. Branches growing out of branches are called secondary branches.

If you decide that a particular branch doesn't agree with your aesthetic, it can be removed by cutting it 1/4" away from the nearest branch junction. After a few days the 'stump' will dry up and can be easily pinched off. (figure 6-2)

Figure 6-2

Training*

It should be noted that training is a highly controversial element of Bonsai Potato™ art. For years the debate has raged about the artistic morality of training. This debate has had a profound impact on the entire art community helping to redefine the meanings of 'aesthetics, morality and obsequious.'

The Purist Viewpoint

Kelli B. Jacobson
S.P.U.D. spokesperson

"True Bonsai Potato™ artists feel that training is a violation of trust in the potato's inner vision. If you choose the potato wisely and help nurture its inner vision through simple pruning and casual conversation, the result will be the most beautiful Bonsai that your individual potato is capable of. The art of the Bonsai Potato™ is part Zen, and Zen is not about total control; it is about symbiosis with your potato."

* Training is an advanced technique which could involve a greater time investment. if you partake in Bonsai Potato™ training it could seriously undermine your "inner-harmony-in-ten-minutes-a-week"goal.

Unfortunately for Bonsai Potato™ purists the modern movement is centered in the United States and the U.S. is about total control, so the purists are becoming the softer voice in the debate.*

The Modern Viewpoint

Jude Lark
Living Art Gallery
New York, NY

"When I look at a potato I know what I want it to do. Sometimes they are incapable of my vision, but with the right encouragement you'd be surprised what a potato can do. I'm not stifling the potato's creativity. Quite the contrary. I am pushing it to its physical limits; encouraging it to become something it never even dreamed it could be. It's tough love. Sometimes it hurts both of us but the end result is unparalleled individuality... and let's face it, the weirder they are the more people are willing to pay for them."

* Though the purist viewpoint of training is less vocal it should be noted that none of the international competitions, and only 20 percent of the U.S. competitions, allow trained entrants.

Composition

The following sections contain advanced Bonsai Potato™ techniques. If you are participating in the Bonsai Potato™ art form as a hobby or to simply cultivate inner peace then composition and training are not critical issues. But if you are serious about promoting progressive Bonsai Potato™ methods or entering U.S. Competition then knowledge of these techniques is a must.

The rules governing Bonsai Potato™ composition are extremely complex. The following is a brief overview and should not be considered a definitive resource.*

Composition Quick Reference Guide

• Every Bonsai Potato™ should have a dominant stalk and at least one secondary stalk. This rule is more semantic than aesthetic. (It stands to reason that there can't be a dominant stalk without one to dominate.)

• Small single stalk clusters should always have an odd number of stalks except when cultivating squid groupings, which should always have ten stalks.

---

* For more information, there is an Australian Aboriginal epic song entitled "Bonsai Potato™ composition: a definitive resourc e ."

• Starburst clusters can have as many individual spikes as they can produce but there should always be at least two smaller supporting clusters and, of those, at least one should be on the same side of the potato as the main cluster.

• Offspring clusters should have no more than 12 individual offspring comprising no more than 22% of the volume of the parent potato.

• In a simple stalk grouping the dominant stalk should not be obscured by the supporting stalks when observed from the prime viewing angle. The exception, of course, is an overlapping secondary root stalk featured in the same visual balance quadrant, or in the case of offspring/starburst combinations.

• Mono-planar, asymmetrical alternating branch stalk formations should contain no more than two secondary stalks, each of which should be no more than 1/4 the height of the dominant stalk. Each ascendant stalk should have no more than two dominant secondary branches, and all subordinate secondary branches should be pruned to a common plane and alternating heights.

For the casual Bonsai Potato™ artist the rules are much simpler.

• Whatever looks good.

Training Methods

Tools you will need
- Thin copper wire
- Wire cutter
- 2 horsepower 3/8"chuck, variable-speed, reversible flange-router (optional)

Once the main stalks and branches have begun to mature it is possible to manipulate their growth patterns to form a more 'aesthetically correct' Bonsai Potato™. This technique uses a combination of wires and external support mechanisms to hold the stalks in place until they permanently adopt the desired shape.

Wiring

Choose the stalk you would like to train. It should be at least three inches long and able to stand on its own. (Thicker stalks will work but there is a greater risk of damaging them if you contort them too much.) Choose a thin copper wire that is not heavy enough to overburden the stalk but is strong enough to retain the desired shape.

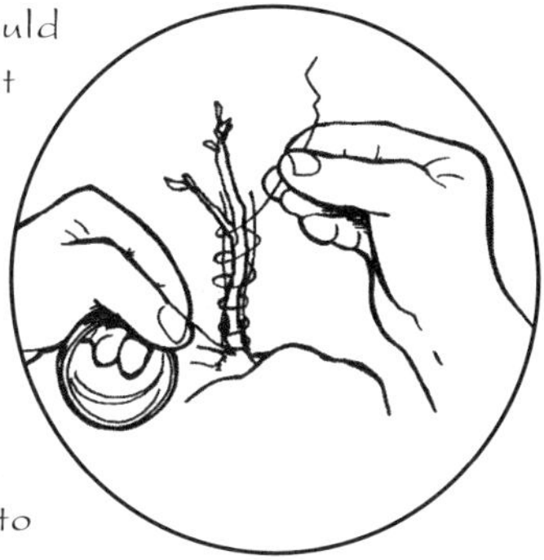

Figure 6-3

Starting at the bottom, wrap your thin copper wire in a clockwise spiral around the stalk. For longer stalks or more intricate manipulation it may be necessary to run two straight lengths of wire up either side of the stalk for added stability before wrapping. (figure 6-3)

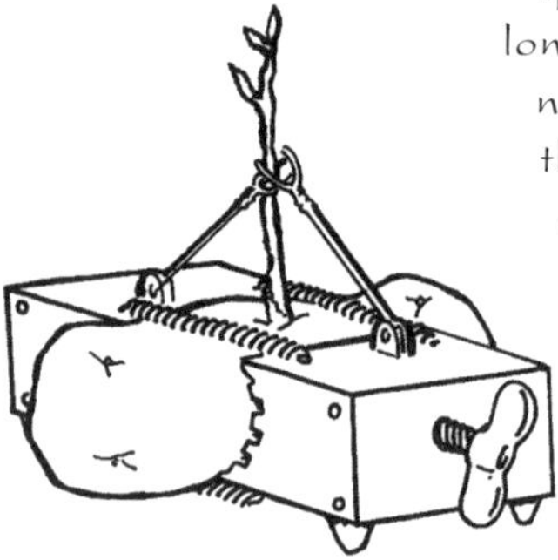

If the stalk you are wiring is long and weak, you may also need to wrap the wire around the body of the potato a couple of times before spiraling up the stalk. If this is not enough, you should use a Spring-pressure neutral growth anchor clamp. (figure 6-4)

Figure 6-4

Once the stalk is firmly stabilized you can begin to bend it. If you are working on a thicker stalk you should bend it a little at a time over a couple of days. Smaller stalks can be bent immediately.

Support Mechanisms

As you add the weight of wire to your stalk and then throw it off natural balance by bending it you may find it necessary to add external support mechanisms to hold the stalk in place until it can grow to hold its own weight. After a few weeks the stalk should be able to support itself and the wire can be carefully removed.

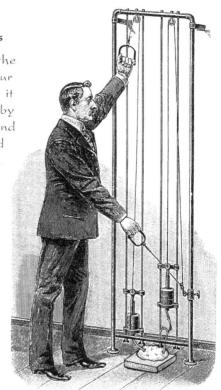

Figure 6-5
Bonsai Potato™ support mechanism circa 1902

Historically, support mechanisms were complex and unwieldy, (figure 6-5) but modern engineering and materials have led to considerable advancements in Bonsai Potato™ support technology. (figures 6-6 & 6-7)

No matter how advanced these technologies become there are people who believe that they do nothing but lead artists to stray from the original intent of

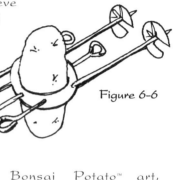

Figure 6-6

Bonsai Potato™ art, which is to realize the inner vision of the potato. This would not be a comprehensive text on Bonsai Potato™ without including them. The extent to which you use them is, of course, up to you.

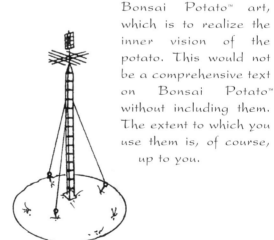

Figure 6-7

A Note on Intimidation

As we all know, sometimes it takes more than physical manipulation to get what we want. This is where old-fashioned psychological torture comes in handy. This should only be used in extreme cases (i.e. your potato isn't doing something you REALLY want it to do). The method is simple. Put your potato in a room, plug in your 2-horsepower 3/8" chuck variable-speed reversible flange router, explain to your potato what you would like it to do, turn on the router and go to a movie. Chances are, when you return your potato will be well on the way to reform.

SECTION 7

Displaying your Bonsai Potato™

This should be an exciting time because you are about to present your Bonsai Potato™ for all to see. You may or may not have put a lot of work into your Bonsai Potato™. Either way you should be proud to show off the vegetable of your labor.

Your Bonsai Potato™ Altar

Included in your Bonsai Potato™ kit is your very own, state-of-the-art, ancient Bonsai Potato™ altar which was created by Master Robert MacDonald, one of the most prolific Bonsai Potato™ artists of ancient Ireland. (See section 1, figure 1-1)

Each potato is an island and your altar is the sea. The altar serves to isolate your potato from its surroundings like a three-dimensional frame around your artwork.

If you did not start your potato on the altar, now is the time to position it there for display.

• Place your altar on a flat, level surface with the ancient inscription facing you.

• Open the plastic bag containing the non-reflective geo-particulate growth support medium and pour evenly into the indented surface of the Bonsai Potato™ altar.

• Place your potato on top of the growth support medium and slowly move it back and forth (pushing down slightly) until the potato is settled and firmly supported.

Once your potato is presentable you need to decide how elaborate your unveiling will be. There are many examples of this process strewn throughout Bonsai Potato™ history, from the three day Druidic ceremonies to the Jewish 'pot mitzvah'.

The modern standard introduction

Prepare your home with subdued lighting and relaxing music.* Invite three to nine of your close friends and family over. If they drink alcohol, a full-bodied red wine would be perfect for the occasion. (A couple of glasses each wouldn't hurt.) Once everyone is relaxed, explain that you have become involved in a recently re-discovered semi-ancient artform and you would like to share with them this important new part of your life.

* Pierre Keating's 'Lamenting Bagpipe Sonata' is perfect for this occasion.

Reach into your closet, pantry, cupboard, or wherever you are growing your potato. Carefully grasp the base and hold it so the inscription is facing away from you. Return to your friends and present them with your Bonsai Potato™!

There is a possibility that even after all this your audience may be unable to fully appreciate (or possibly even partially comprehend) your Bonsai Potato™.

If your friends insist that you are nuts, tell them that you were just kidding and that you are actually doing government research on micro-gravity hydroponics for a secret space station being built by the U.S. and Japan.

Pick up your altar (explaining that it is a Japanese micro-gravity simulator), put it away, and ask that your 'friends' not mention it to anyone for obvious national security reasons.

If you do clear the hurdle of social acceptance you can bring your potato out of the closet for special occasions. Holiday, dinner parties, birthdays etc. are all great times to show off your growing artistic relationship with your potato.

Note: Unlike normal relationships, this one will develop better if kept in the dark. Although being out in the open will do no immediate harm to your Bonsai Potato™, it does prefer darkness. So for optimum growth potential, it is wise to ration display exposure.

"For every hill you climb, there is one to descend."

- Zen proverb

SECTION 8

Documenting your Bonsai

The art of the Bonsai Potato™ will enable you to condense decades of enjoyment into a few months. The disadvantage to this reality is that just as your relationship seems richest, your Bonsai Potato™ having expended it's life energy on the grand opus of artistic expression, will die. (See Section 9: The Cycle of Life.)

Knowing this ahead of time, however, gives you the opportunity to live every moment with your potato to the fullest.

Many people, realizing that their potato will not always be around, choose to somehow document their Bonsai Potato™. In this way they create a legacy and form a deeper connection with their potato.

This section highlights examples of Bonsai Potato™ artwork. Through Haiku, painting, drawing, dancing and, more recently photography, people have expressed to themselves and the world the profound connection they feel with their Bonsai Potato™.

Portrait of Ferdinand
Queen Charlotte III 1793

"untitled"
Danny Ostensa
Blacksmith 1812

"Coat of Arms – d'Arby clan"
circa 1520
Artist unknown

"self portrait"
Sir Isaac Newton, 1660

HAIKU

at autumn's last light
fair tuber of my labors
shriveled, greets the night

- Jane Lillith

have you enemy
your glow is ever present
tell them you are loved

- Leftenant Murdock the Stunted
Mongolian Imperial Reserve Navy 1911

your eyes filled with dirt
and mine with bittersweet tears
I will not forget

- W.T. Faulkner 1948

Painters, philosophers, poets, postal employees, and people from all walks of life and levels of artistic proficiency have preserved, and continue to preserve the spirits of their Bonsai Potatoes™ for future generations.

SECTION 9

The Cycle of Life
or Letting Go of your Bonsai Potato™

In the autumn of your Bonsai Potato's™ life you will begin to notice some changes. The most obvious are the physical ones. The stalk growth will begin to look much like a rock. Your potato will have accomplished its primary artistic vision and is now developing "character." Unfortunately there is a fine line between having character and being dead.

Emotionally, your potato will gradually become lethargic, then listless, and finally totally unresponsive. Bonsai Potatoes™ are subject to bouts of depression or angst during their developmental period, but this is much more extreme.

Soon your Bonsai Potato™ will simply cease to function. It is now time to pass it on to the afterworld. There are a number of ways to do this.

Note: A normal Bonsai Potato™ will wither away gracefully, but if you notice a strange odor or nonstandard growth patterns (i.e. mold) you should dispose of your potato immediately. Fortunately, this is extremely rare since it is difficult when you have come to know and trust your potato. But some potatoes have latent, evil tendencies which manifest in the final stages of life.

Managing The Remains

Garbage - Throwing the remains of your Bonsai Potato™ in the garbage is considered by many to be the least reverent, but most popular option. If you look at your potato as nothing more than a physical vessel then this is the most pragmatic solution. Cherish the memory not the carcass.

Cremation - If you choose cremation you can always have the ashes of your favorite Bonsai Potato™ with you, or you can return them to the earth. The art of the Bonsai Potato™ has only recently been reintroduced into world culture, so Bonsai Potato™ crematoriums are still fairly rare, through within a matter of years they will be in every major city.

Go camping, build a fire, wrap your Bonsai Potato™ in heavy duty aluminum foil, set it in the fire and wait. Within hours you will have a charred bundle containing the ashes of your potato. The regulations on spreading potato ashes are still very lax so you should be able to spread them wherever you think your potato would like to rest. (You will need a permit in certain parts of Utah.) Home cremation is also possible, but it involves a broiler and a fire extinguisher and is not recommended.

Burial - This involves digging a small hole in a special spot (preferably a spot you are allowed to be digging in), placing your deceased potato in the hole, and covering it with dirt. Bonsai Potato™ burial often has the ironic result of creating life. The potato produces a plant which produces more potatoes. This is the perfect way to pass on the traits of a particularly creative Bonsai Potato™. This type of lineage preservation is also required in purebred divisions of Bonsai Potato™ shows.

Cryonics - This is a fairly modern option which involves quickly freezing the expired potato and maintaining it in suspended animation until medical technology advances to the point that it can cure whatever it was that caused death. The potato can then be revived and cured. The revival of humans isn't even possible yet and medical potato research is extremely under-funded. In the future, potato-medical research will certainly become an important field, but it may still be a way of. Cryonics solves the problem of time by suspending it indefinitely.

The disadvantage of cryonic suspension is the extreme expense of freezing and storing your potato. A state of the art cryonics lab would charge nearly $15,000 just for the liquid nitrogen freezing process, and storage runs over $1,200 per year. Many people are deciding to take matters into their own homes by using household freezers. This may seem morbid to some, but would cost only pennies per year. The freezing process is less sophisticated, but if technology advances to where they can cure death, then freezer burn shouldn't be much of a hurdle.

Note: Flushing, though common with goldfish, is not recommended for your Bonsai Potato™.

In the late 1500's in Ireland there are records from elaborate ceremonies to honor the passing of Bonsai Potatoes™. These observances involved music, dancing, food and fire, and would often last for days. Due to the lifespan of the average Bonsai Potato™ many clans became impoverished because of the frequent, elaborate and expensive ceremonies. Since this time, disposal ceremonies have become private affairs involving only the immediate family.

Once your potato is gone you must remember that it was only a physical manifestation of the true essence of your Bonsai Potato™. What you have now is infinitely more valuable than the potato itself. You have a memory. Over time your memory will become more precious.

> "Nostalgia fogs the pasture of memory until
> only the luminous sensations are visible."
>
> – Emma Coates
> English poetess

We live in the world of memories. As individuals we are formed by the memory of our experiences. Even something as powerful and romantic as the night sky is nothing more than a memory. Light from a distant star can take millions of years to reach Earth. Therefore, it is possible (if not likely) that many of the stars we stare at with our true love on a warm summer night no longer exist, destroyed a million years before their last illumination reached the Earth. But we are still mesmerized by the ancient light.

Dealing with grief – don't forget the ancient illumination of your Bonsai Potato™ but use this time to renew the cycle of life. Begin working on a previously started Bonsai Potato™ or start a new one. Either way, it's a good idea to jump back on the proverbial horse. Soon you will develop a new relationship, but you can still cherish the old one.

Folk musician Tennessee Mark wrote in his song "October Moon",

"...the past is a wonderful place to visit but I wouldn't want to live there . "

Glossary of Terms

Altar – An ancient support container used to display a Bonsai Potato™.

Baby Red – Small potatoes, usually red in color.

Bonsai – The art of stunting trees through the use of specialized pruning techniques.

Bonsai Potato™– The art of nurturing the artistic expression of a potato through various forms of encouragement and manipulation.

Branch – Growth radiating from a main stalk.

China – Vitrified crockery.

Composition – Strict rules governing the arrangement and appearance of Bonsai Potato™ growth.

Evil Potato – A potato with a malicious artistic vision

Inner peace – A harmonious life-force balance resulting in a severe anxiety deficiency.

Juvenile bud – Small tightly packed leaves indicating the first growths of a new stalk or branch.

Moon Ladder – A Bonsai Potato™ grouping consisting of a dominant stalk with left and right alternating ascending branches.

Non-reflective geo-particulate growth support medium – Black gravel.

Offspring cluster – A Bonsai Potato™ grouping consisting of small secondary potatoes growing in bunches on the surface of a parent or host potato.

Potato – Duh.

Pruning – Selectively eliminating growth to influence the shape of a Bonsai Potato™.

Root stalk – A main stalk which originates from the underside of the potato.

Russet – Quick sprouting and hearty, the Russet is the most common Bonsai Potato™ starter potato.

S.P.U.D. – Society for the Promotion of Useless Diversions.

A Bonsai Potato™ purist advocacy group.

Secondary branch – A growth emanating from a main stalk or a main branch.

Simple stalk – A single straight stalk with little or no secondary branches.

Simple stalk grouping – An organization of two or more single stalk potatoes to form a multi-potato arrangement.

Spring-pressure neutral growth anchor clamp – Duh.

Squid grouping – A cluster with 5-12 single (or simple) stalks each over 6" in length.

Stalk – A primary growth emanating from the surface of the potato.

Starburst cluster – A Bonsai Potato™ grouping featuring tightly packed short stalks (spikes) emerging from a single point.

Training – A controversial method of manipulating the artistic vision of a Bonsai Potato™ through wire bondage and psychological torture.

Wiring – The process of using malleable wire to hold Bonsai Potato™ growths in a particular position until they grow to support themselves

Yukon gold – Golden medium sized potatoes which are slow to start but create beautifully colored stalks.

Zen – See Zen.

"Patience is a virtue"

- Anonymous

"Not everyone is virtuous"

- Anonymous

Appendix A

Meat and Potatoes
Bonsai Potato™ Quick Reference Guide

Traditional bonsai trees can take hundreds of years to mature. The trees are passed down through and cared for by many generations. The art of the Bonsai Potato™ provides an opportunity to benefit from the creation of bonsai without the outrageous time investment.

For some, even this isn't good enough. You need to have satisfaction NOW! You know who you are (you're probably only skimming this paragraph). STOP! Here's what you're looking for. The absolute bare bones guide to the art of the Bonsai Potato™ with handy reference to chapters for further research.

Bonsai Potato™
Quick Reference Guide

• Pick out a potato. (See section 3: Choosing your potato).

• Put the potato on your Bonsai Potato™ altar.

• Find a warm, dark spot for your potato.

• When stalks and branches appear, prune to taste. Use tweezers to remove unwanted buds and prevent overgrowth. Cut off unwanted branches or stalks 1/4" from base. In a few days pinch off the dead stump. (See Section 6: Pruning and Training.)

•Present it to your friends and family. (See Section 7: Displaying your Bonsai Potato™.)

• Bask in your new-found sense of tranquility and inner harmony.

Bonsai Potato™
Quick Reference Guide
abridged version

• Get a potato.

• Put it on the base.

• Put it in the dark.

• Wait.

• Enjoy.

Surrogate Bonsai Potato™

If you are still unable to wait for results we have enclosed a surrogate Bonsai Potato™. This will provide you with the illusion of accomplishment until you can actually achieve it. Consider it a Zen credit card. Cut it out, pour the gravel in the altar and prop your surrogate potato up using the gravel to stabilize it. This should serve as a reasonable facsimile until your real Bonsai Potato™ is ready.

Appendix B

What am I Doing Wrong?
Common Bonsai Potato™ Mistakes

If something is going wrong, don't take it personally. Remember, you are helping the potato, so if something isn't working it's not your fault. It's the potato's fault.

All that you need to do is make sure you didn't accidentally get an evil potato. (See "Be the Potato" in Section 2.)

If you determine that your potato is evil, dispose of it immediately. In my experience, evil potatoes can have a significant influence on other potatoes so it would be a good idea to quarantine and individually re-examine the motives of all the potatoes in your growing area.

Note: The old adage that "one bad apple can spoil the whole bunch" originated in Ireland as a Gaelic proverb about potatoes, which were commonly referred to as ground apples.

"Choose your path wisely and let the potato lead the way."

- Robert MacDonald
Bonsai Potato™ master

Legalese

The author recognizes that there are regulations governing the use of trademarks. In order to maintain the integrity of a given trademark it is important to not use it as a generic term. Throughout this book there are many examples of the trademarked words Bonsai Potato™ being used improperly.

On a cool spring evening, In April of 1958, a terrorist organization known to the world as Four for Fauxr took over a bus station in Denver, Colorado. They held 42 people hostage for almost two weeks. After numerous rounds of harrowing negotiations, 39 of the hostages were released unharmed. Of the remaining hostages, one suffered permanent amnesia, one required extensive hemorrhoid surgery and the remaining hostage joined Jour for Fauxr and refused to leave.

One week before this text was to go to press we were approached by the FBI. Evidently, buried deep within the hostage release agreement was an obscure paragraph. Section 5/ sub-section 14/45.2.13 reads:

Any future text pertaining to or referring to any form of recreational horticulture involving vegetables (specifically tubers) intended for publication in any medium including, but not limited to books, magazines, newspapers, fortune cookies and multi-media not yet conceived of throughout the universe and in perpetuity shall, through improper usage, intentionally jeopardize any trademarked terms, phrases, logos or gestures in order to protect future interests of Four for Fauxr.

We were forced to change this text to comply with the terrorist's wishes. Therefore the improper usage in this book is acknowledged and disclaimed as compliant with federal law regulating terrorist negotiation integrity.

This book is based on actual fictitious accounts. The names of the characters have been changed to protect the fact that they never existed.

The Art of the Bonsai Potato™ KIT is not recommended for children

The Art of the Bonsai Potato™ KIT is not recommended for people who are likely to eat rocks